D0650004

SYDNEY & SIMON
Full STEAM Ahead!

STORY BY PAUL A. REYNOLDS ART BY PETER H. REYNOLDS

ıпı Charlesbridge

*To all creative educators who support
the arts and make an enduring impact
on the lives of their students*
—*P. A. R.*

*To our mother, Hazel, for surrounding her
twin boys with art supplies and monthly
mail-order science activity kits, sparking
our love for exploration and discovery*
—*P. H. R.*

Text copyright © 2014 by Paul A. Reynolds
Illustrations copyright © 2014 by Peter H. Reynolds

Published by Charlesbridge
85 Main Street
Watertown, MA 02472
(617) 926-0329
www.charlesbridge.com

Library of Congress Cataloging-in-Publication Data
Reynolds, Paul A.
  Sydney & Simon: full steam ahead!/Paul A. Reynolds; illustrated by Peter H. Reynolds.
     p. cm.
  Summary: Twins Sydney and Simon learn about the water cycle and use science,
technology, engineering, arts, and math to solve the problem of their stuck window
and thirsty flowers.
  ISBN 978-1-58089-675-7 (reinforced for library use)
  ISBN 978-1-60734-750-7 (ebook)
  ISBN 978-1-60734-693-7 (ebook pdf)
1. Twins—Juvenile fiction. 2. Brothers and sisters—Juvenile fiction. 3. Critical thinking—
Juvenile fiction. 4. Hydrologic cycle—Juvenile fiction. [1. Twins—Fiction. 2. Brothers
and sisters—Fiction. 3. Experiments—Fiction. 4. Water—Fiction.] I. Reynolds, Peter,
1961–illustrator. II. Title. III. Title: Sydney & Simon. IV. Title: Full steam ahead!
PZ7.R337645Sv 2014
813.54—dc23   2013038221

Printed in Singapore
(hc) 10 9 8 7 6 5 4 3 2 1

Illustrations created with ink, watercolor wash, Parisian water, and tea
Display type set in Chowderhead by Font Diner
Text typeset in Schneidler BT by Bitstream Inc.
Color separations by KHL Chroma Graphics, Singapore
Printed and bound February 2014 by Imago in Singapore
Production supervision by Brian G. Walker
Reynolds Studio supervision by Julia Anne Young
Designed by Diane M. Earley

Contents

1
Stuck with a Problem

Hot, hot, hot! It was another steamy summer morning in Wonder Falls. Sydney and Simon Starr sat under the kitchen fan and tried to stay cool.

"Our big flower show is next week," Sydney announced, holding up her poster. "I hope we win first prize."

"Not so fast, Syd," replied her twin brother, Simon. "If our flowers don't get more water, they will never last until the competition."

About two months before, the Starr family
planted seeds in the window box outside their
third-floor apartment. The spring rains helped the
seeds sprout quickly.

But when a heat wave hit last week, the soil in
the window box became dry—very dry. To make
matters worse, the window was now stuck.

Sydney and Simon tried and tried to open it.
Even when they gave it their double-push twin
power, the window still wouldn't budge.

The twins had been planning the neighborhood
Art in Bloom show all year. Sydney wanted to
share the flowers she had grown and the ones she
had drawn. Simon wanted to finish his video. He
had been filming how the flowers were planted and
cared for.

But with no way to water the flowers, Sydney
and Simon had a big problem.

Simon could see his sister growing worried about the flowers.

"Hey, Syd," he said. "Just remember the Starr family motto: *When the going gets tough, the creative get going!*"

Sydney wanted to figure out a creative rescue plan, but she felt as stuck as that old window.

An idea came to Simon. "Follow me," he said and rushed out the door.

Sydney ran after him. Outside in their backyard they could see their kitchen window and the flower box high above.

"Let's try the hose," Simon suggested.

The faucet squeaked when Sydney turned the handle, and the garden hose wiggled as water pulsed through it. Simon aimed straight up toward the flowers, but the flow of water wasn't strong enough.

Instead of reaching the flowers, the water came splashing down on Simon's head.

Sydney laughed. "Too bad we didn't get that on video! Before we try anything else," she said, "let's do some *thinkering*."

Simon gave her a funny look. "Syd, *thinkering* isn't a word."

"It is now," Sydney declared. "I've just invented it, and I'm going to add it to my Wonder Journal."

2
All Steamed Up!

Back in the kitchen Sydney drew pictures of
the wilting flowers and the just-won't-budge
window in her Wonder Journal. This was where
she kept her wonderings, artwork, predictions,
and observations. Simon kept an electronic
Wonder Journal filled with video games he made,
music he recorded, and videos he filmed.

"Did the window ever stick like this before?"
Sydney asked Simon.

On his tablet Simon found a funny photo of their
mom making a something-smells-really-bad face.

"When we tried our stinky rotten-egg experiment
last winter, we opened the windows really fast!"

"Does that mean the hot weather could be causing the windows to stick?" Sydney asked. She *did* believe the weather had something to do with it, and so she wrote down this hypothesis under "Bunches of Hunches." Making predictions helped Sydney explain what she was thinking.

Just then Mrs. Starr walked in holding one of her latest inventions.

"Hi, Mom," Sydney said. "Simon and I are wondering why the windows open so easily when the weather is cool but not when the weather is hot."

Mrs. Starr was an inventor. She loved science, and just like Sydney and Simon, she was always asking questions and searching for answers. "How might warm weather be able to do that?" Mrs. Starr asked. "What's your hunch?"

Sydney's eyes brightened. "Well, it's been hot but it's also been really humid. Humidity is the amount of water vapor in the air, right, Mom?"

Mrs. Starr replied, "Well, what do you think?"

"I don't see any water vapor in the air." Simon wrinkled his nose.

Sydney reminded her brother that the tiny water drops—or water vapor—that make up humidity are invisible. "We can only see water vapor when it's cooling down."

Mr. Starr came into the kitchen to pull his steaming kettle off the stove. He was writing his latest poetry book. Even in the middle of a heat wave, Mr. Starr needed a tea break.

"So that steam is actually water vapor cooling down when it leaves the kettle?" Simon asked.

"I think so," said Sydney. "Maybe this same sort of thing happens any time water gets really hot." She and Simon decided to investigate.

"Full *steam* ahead!" called Simon.

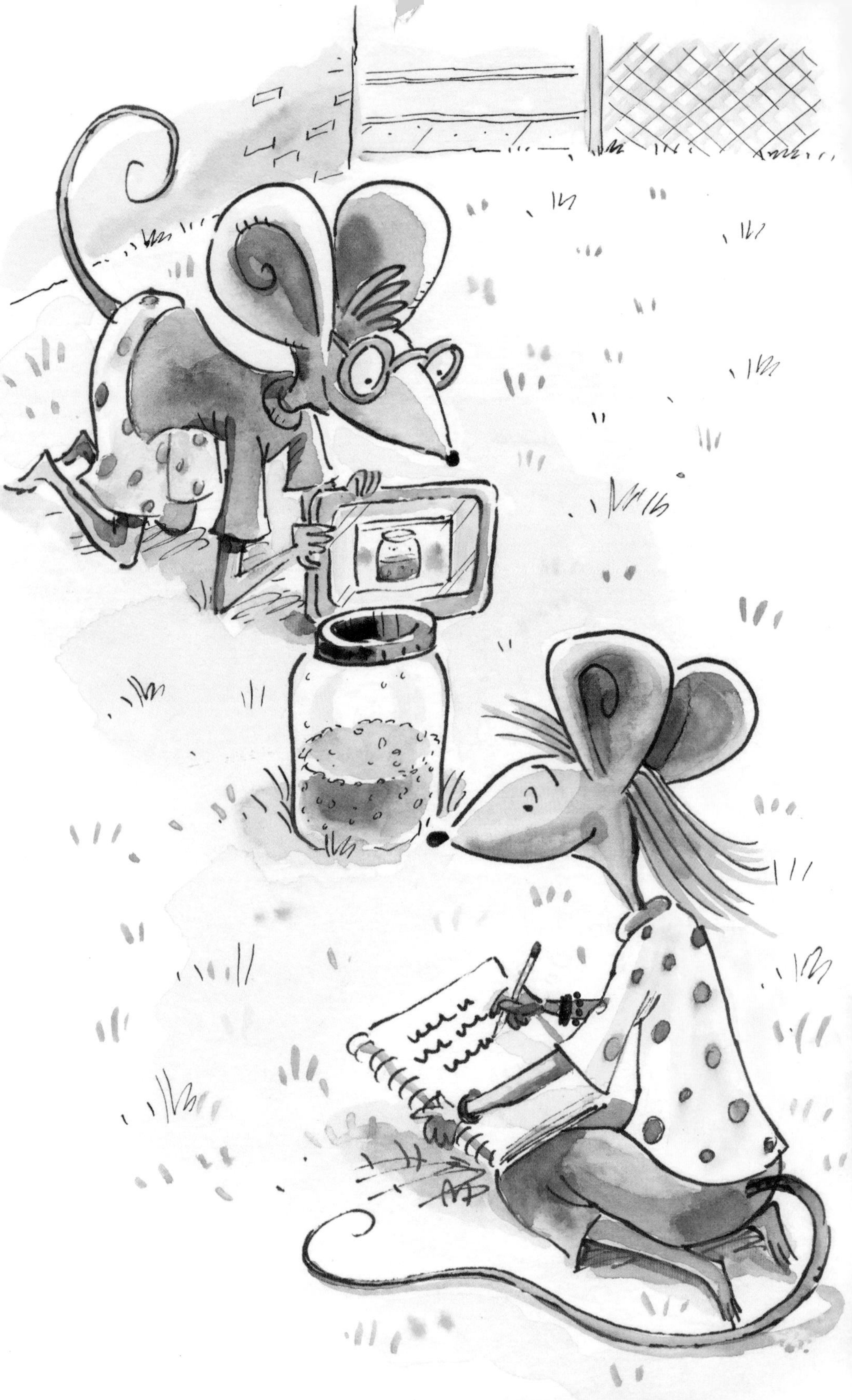

3

A Jarring Conclusion

After planning their experiment Sydney and Simon marched into the backyard. They filled a glass jar halfway with dirt and added five spoonfuls of water. Simon took a picture with his tablet.

"This is the *before* picture," he explained.

They put the lid on the jar and placed it in the hot sun.

Sydney drew her version of a *before* picture. Drawing made her ideas easier to understand and share.

"I predict we'll see evidence of the water escaping the dirt, just like the steam escaped from Dad's kettle," she said.

"I predict I'll need some iced tea after we're finished in this hot sun!" Simon announced.

The jar sat in the sun all afternoon. Eventually the sides of the jar steamed up, and big drops of water rolled down the inside of the glass. Simon took another picture.

"This is the *after* picture," he said. They made note of how different the jar looked now compared to when they first set it in the sun.

The twins ran inside to tell their parents what happened.

"The water in the dirt got so hot it evaporated into the air inside the jar," Simon reported. "Just like the water heating up in Dad's teakettle evaporated, too."

Sydney described how the water evaporating from the kettle became steam. But since the jar had a lid on it, the steam couldn't escape. Instead, it clumped together and formed big droplets. The droplets rolled down the inside of the jar and fell back into the soil—like rain.

"If the sun heats up the soil again, the same thing will happen all over," Simon noted.

"You have just described the water cycle!"
Mr. Starr was quite proud.

"Really?" asked Simon. "But what does this
dirt-in-the-jar experiment tells us about our
stuck window?"

"I think that the water vapor in the air hasn't
turned into rain yet, so it's adding to the humidity,"
said Sydney. "The dry wood around the glass is
sucking up that water vapor and expanding. It's
like a sponge that gets bigger when it soaks up
water. Now the window is too fat to be pushed up
the swollen frame it's sitting in."

"Humidity is pretty sneaky," said Simon.

It was helpful to know why the window was stuck. But this didn't make it any less stuck. Simon could see his sister worrying about the drooping flowers again.

"Don't worry, Sydney." Simon pointed to a weather report on his tablet. "Look, cooler weather is on its way. We shouldn't be stuck and out of luck much longer."

4
The Leaky Problem

The next day Sydney and Simon were back in the kitchen. The weather report was right. It was eight degrees cooler than the day before.

The twins pushed up on the window again. And again. *Skkrrr-erkkk!* This time it actually opened about two inches. They guessed that there was less humidity in the air—and in the window.

"Woo-hoo!" shouted Simon.

But the opening turned out to be too small. The spout of their watering can wouldn't fit through it.

"Maybe we should just forget about entering our flowers in the show," Sydney said sadly.

"*Shhhh!* Did you hear that?" Simon suddenly asked.

Drip! Drip! Ploink!

Water was dripping from the kitchen faucet.

The drips had a great beat. Simon counted them.

"I can add a melody to the rhythm of the drips
and write a song for the flower show," he
explained. He started recording with his tablet.
They still had a stuck window, but that didn't
make Simon any less curious about the dripping
noise. Creative connections were everywhere.

Sydney looked concerned. "Sounds like water is
being wasted to me."

"Syd, they're just little drips," Simon said.

"Sure, but little drips add up over time," Sydney explained.

"So let's save them," Simon said. "We can give the water to our flowers when we open the window all the way."

"Great idea!" said Sydney.

She put an empty one-gallon milk jug under the faucet and glanced at the clock. "I predict that before tomorrow, the jug will almost be full."

"I predict that before then, I'll record a song for the show!" Simon snapped to the beat of the drips.

"*If* we have a show." Sydney sighed.

In the next twenty-four hours, the drips nearly filled the jug.

"Wow!" said Simon. "Those little drips add up."

"What if the faucet dripped for the whole year? How much water would that be?" Sydney asked.

Simon put the cap on the jug and put another empty jug under the faucet. "I know someone else who would want to know about all this wasted water."

Sydney took a guess. "Uncle Rusty?"

"Right! Two minds, one twin thought!" Simon said, and they headed out the door toward Wonder Falls Public Water Department.

5

Picture This

When Sydney and Simon arrived at the water department, Uncle Rusty was in his office. "What's going on, kids?" He was a busy engineer, but he put down his blueprint with a big smile for his niece and nephew.

"Uncle Rusty, the problems are really flowing this week," Simon started. They told him about their partially open, still-stuck window; their droopy flowers; their leaky faucet; and how much wasted water they had collected.

Uncle Rusty looked alarmed. "I hate leaks. After all we do here to move water from the reservoir to Wonder Falls, it makes me crazy to hear when it's wasted."

"Us, too," said Sydney. She was eyeing the whiteboard on Uncle Rusty's wall. It looked like the perfect place to draw pictures.

"Mom and Dad are trying to fix the leak," Simon said. "But they may need your help."

"When the weather is this hot, we need every drop of water we can get," Sydney remarked.

She and Simon shared what they knew from their own leaky-faucet observations. The bar graph they drew on the whiteboard showed how their faucet leaked one gallon of water in one day, which could add up to a lot of wasted water in one month.

"All that wasted water could feed all the flowers at the show for a long time." Sydney observed.

Simon quickly searched the internet on his tablet. "Did you know it takes about thirty-six gallons of water to fill a bathtub?" he asked.

"Until we fix our faucet, maybe I should take one less bath a month," Simon joked.

Uncle Rusty smiled. "I wish I could help with your other water wonderings, kids, but I should get back to planning my big project."

Sydney and Simon were curious.

"I'm building a system of pumps and pipes," Uncle Rusty explained. "They will bring water to Wonder Falls from a new, bigger reservoir. Then we'll make sure the water gets cleaned up and pumped from here to every faucet in town."

Sydney and Simon looked at each other with a quick, at-the-same-time twin glance. "That's it! We need our own water-pumping plan," Simon declared.

"Uncle Rusty, we'll let you get back to your planning," Sydney said. She and Simon began chatting about a way to make a pump that would get water through the small opening in their window.

"I know someone who would love to hear about our idea to make a pump," said Sydney.

The twins set off for Wonder Falls Elementary.

When they got to their school, Sydney and Simon found their science teacher, Ms. Fractalini. She ran the summer theater program and had told them to stop by anytime.

"Ms. Fractalini, we've got a problem to tackle," Simon began.

The twins told her about their wilting flowers and how they wanted to make a flower-rescue pump.

"That's great! I absolutely *love* problems!" she exclaimed. "I find that most can be solved with creative thinking," she told them. "Or STEAM thinking: using Science, Technology, Engineering,

Arts, and Math to imagine new discoveries and to see the creative connections between all subjects.

"Building a water pump will certainly need this kind of thinking. Did you know that Leonardo da Vinci was an engineer who invented all sorts of water machines, like pumps, waterwheels, and even a water-powered clock?"

"He was also a fabulous painter," added Sydney.

"That's right," said Ms. Fractalini. "Leonardo da Vinci studied and mastered many subjects. He explored what other people had invented before him, then designed new ideas and tried them out."

"That's the *art* of invention," Simon added.

"And the art of *inspiration*," Ms. Fractalini said. "Leonardo was inspired by the screw pump, a water pump invented by Archimedes. He was a Greek mathematician and inventor who lived nearly 1,800 years before Leonardo."

Two inventors who had never even met had worked on the same problem. Sydney thought that was pretty neat.

Simon began looking up information about the Archimedes screw pump. After talking to Ms. Fractalini, he and Sydney had more ideas of their own.

6
From Wondering to Wonderful

Back at home the twins sketched out their own Archimedes model. They gathered a long empty plastic bottle, a tube, and some tape. They wrapped the tube around the bottle. Before long they had built a screw pump.

"Don't forget," said Sydney, "we have to use the water we saved from the leaky faucet." She and Simon poured the water into a bowl.

Sydney turned the screw pump in the bowl. The opening in the tube at the bottom of the pump scooped up the water.

With each turn of the pump, the tube scooped more water, and the water climbed up the tube. The pump was like a spiral winding ramp. Usually water flows downward because of gravity. But the pump kept pushing water up and up until it came out the tube at the top of the bottle. Through the small opening in the window, the dry dirt in the flower box got a drink at last.

"It's working!" squealed Sydney. She turned the screw pump until the flowers had plenty to drink.

"The flowers will recover quickly now," said Mr. Starr as he helped Mrs. Starr fix the leaky faucet. "And your water pump has given me an idea for a science poem."

"Just make sure you give credit to Archimedes," Simon insisted. "He inspired us to create our water pump."

"Maybe your poem will inspire others to do some *thinkering* about pumps, too," Sydney said.

About a week later it was time for the Art in Bloom Show at last. Cooler weather all week meant the twins could open the window all the way and bring in the flowers. Now the Starr family's flowers were proudly and colorfully on display.

Sydney shared her artwork. She thought her sketches were easy to read, like Uncle Rusty's neat blueprints.

Simon had finished his video about their sticky-wilty-drippy-leaky-pumped-up problem-solving adventure. He got a kick out of seeing everyone dance to his dripping-water song.

Just as the video was ending, dark clouds rolled in and rain started to sprinkle down.

Everyone covered the artwork.

Everyone ran inside . . .

. . . everyone but Sydney and Simon.

The twins did a little rain dance as the shower washed over them. "The show went on after all!" Sydney exclaimed.

"Thanks to our teamwork," Simon said proudly. "I can't wait for our next big discovery."

Then, with a double-twin-size shout, they both called out, "Full STEAM ahead!"

Glossary

Archimedes—a Greek physicist, engineer, mathematician, inventor, and astronomer who lived from 287–212 BCE. He is credited with designing groundbreaking machines, including the screw pump.

art—something (like a painting, drawing, song, or sculpture) that is created with imagination, is beautiful, or that shows important ideas or feelings

bar graph—a picture that uses columns or bars of different lengths to show amounts, making it easier to get an overall idea of which amounts are more or less than the others

blueprint—a drawing or print of white lines on a blue background that details a plan for something that will be made, such as a building or an invention

engineering—the work of creating and designing large structures (such as bridges or pipes) by engineers (people who apply science and math to make engines or machines)

evaporation—the process of turning from a liquid into a gas, becoming a vapor

evidence—a sign that shows something is true

experiment—a scientific test performed and carefully observed in order to discover something

gravity—the natural force that causes physical things to move toward each other

heat wave—a period of unusually hot weather

humidity—invisible moisture in the air

hypothesis—an idea or theory that is not yet proven but that may lead to further study

inspiration—an idea that makes someone want to do or create something

invention—an original device, machine, or method created by someone (the inventor)

Leonardo da Vinci—an Italian painter, sculptor, architect, musician, mathematician, engineer, inventor, and writer. He lived from 1452–1519 and is credited as one of the most talented painters and inventors of all time.

math—the science of numbers, shapes, and quantities and the relations between them

melody—musical notes arranged in a specific order to make a pleasing song

observation—something you notice by watching and listening

prediction—a guess of what will happen next

ramp—a sloping surface that leads from one level to another

reservoir—a man-made lake where communities collect and store water to use in their homes, schools, and businesses

rhythm—a regular repeating pattern of sounds or movements, like the dripping of a faucet or the beating of a drum

science—information about or the study of the natural world based on facts learned through observations and experiments

screw pump—a pump that rotates with a tube-shaped opening, moving fluids or solids along the pump's screw or screwlike spindle

steam—the hot gas that is created when water is boiled

technology—the use of science in industry or engineering to help solve problems or invent useful things

thinkering—Sydney's word for a combination of "thinking" and "tinkering" when using your imagination or experimenting

water cycle—the constant movement of the Earth's water because of evaporation, condensation, and precipitation

water vapor—a gas form of water, usually produced by evaporation

Are You a STEAM Thinker?

Dear Readers:

Writing and illustrating books about Sydney and Simon is fun for us because we're super-curious twins, too! Being curious is exciting. In fact, being curious can make you a **STEAM** thinker. What's that, you ask?

STEAM stands for Science, Technology, Engineering, Arts, and Math. **STEAM** thinkers look for breakthrough ideas and creative connections across all these subjects and beyond. Like Sydney and Simon, they solve problems, innovate, invent, share ideas, and celebrate the things that make our world fascinating. Discovering **STEAM** thinking means discovering how subjects overlap. In science you can use art to draw a diagram or record results. In engineering or building you can use math to figure out how angles or shapes fit together. And with technology you can experiment within all sorts of subjects: for example, you can use computers to make music, build 3-D graphics of buildings, construct mathematical graphs, or study satellite images of outer space.

We're especially interested in how the arts fit into **STEAM** thinking. Drawing, designing, sculpting, writing, music, dance, theater, and many other art forms are great ways to show what you know. As the author and illustrator of this book, we shared ideas about Science, Technology, Engineering, and Math through the *Art* of writing and illustrating.

Next time you use the arts in connection with Science, Technology, Engineering, or Math, tell us about it. We want to hear YOUR stories! **www.steamthinking.org**

Your **STEAM**-powered friends,

PAUL & PETER